Walt Disney's
Mickey Mouse
and the Lucky Goose Chase

A GOLDEN BOOK · NEW YORK
Western Publishing Company, Inc., Racine, Wisconsin 53404

"Time to get Sweetheart ready for the contest," Farmer Mickey Mouse said to Morty and Ferdie. They all went to the pen where Sweetheart, the boys' pet calf, lived.

They found Commander, a big goose, hovering about. He spread his wings and rushed at Mickey. "Go away, you pesky goose!" Mickey shouted.

Morty and Ferdie worked all morning. They washed and combed Sweetheart's coat until it shined. They polished her hooves. They oiled her halter.

Finally Sweetheart was ready to go to the County Fair.

After lunch, Minnie arrived. "Hi, Minnie," said Mickey. "What's in that basket? Is it cherry pie?"

"Yes," said Minnie. "But you can't have any now. These pies are for the contest at the fair."

It was time to take Sweetheart to the fair. Morty led the calf up the truck's ramp.

Commander strolled up the ramp, too. When Mickey tried to get him out of the truck, he spread his wings and hissed. Mickey backed away.

"All right, you can come along with Sweetheart," he said. "But you have to behave yourself at the fair!"

Commander answered with a honk.

Morty and Ferdie were thrilled to be at the fair. They saw tents being set up. They saw sheep, pigs, and cows being unloaded from vans.

"Come on, boys," said Mickey, "let's get Sweetheart unloaded."

Mickey led the little calf into her stall. Commander marched in, too.

When Mickey put some hay down, Commander pecked at his shoe. Then he knocked over a bucket of water. "Stop it!" Mickey cried.

"I wish you had left that goose at home," Minnie said.

"Me, too," said Mickey.

The next morning Mickey, Minnie, Morty, and Ferdie got a horrible surprise when they returned to the barn. The stall door was open.

"Oh, no!" said Mickey, "Sweetheart has gotten out! Quick! Let's look for her. Maybe we can find her in time for the contest."

Minnie ran to look around the game booths.
Sweetheart was nowhere to be found.

Morty and Ferdie looked near the amusement rides. There was no sign of Sweetheart.

Mickey looked in the animal pens. He saw a tail just like Sweetheart's. He pulled and he pulled...

...but it was the wrong tail!

Minnie, Mickey, Morty, and Ferdie met in the middle of the fairgrounds. Morty and Ferdie were crying.

"We'll never find her in time," Ferdie wailed.

Suddenly they heard a squawk from behind a cotton candy stand.

COTTON
CANDY

"That sounds like Commander," cried Mickey.
"It is!" exclaimed Minnie. "And look who he
is leading!"

The little calf was covered with grain and molasses. She was a sticky mess!

"Sweetheart, you bad calf! How did you get into the feed room?" groaned Mickey.

"We'll never get her cleaned up in time for the contest," said Morty.

"Oh, yes we will," said Mickey. "Quick, let's get started!"

So they all took Sweetheart back to her stall. First, they hosed her down and washed her. Then they brushed her coat until it shined once again.

"Come on," said Mickey, "let's get Sweetheart to the judging area. We'll just make it!"

When Donald, Daisy, Huey, Dewey, and Louie arrived for the fair, they were just in time to see Sweetheart win a blue ribbon for first prize in the calf contest.

"Commander deserves a blue ribbon, too," said Mickey. "If it weren't for him, Sweetheart would have missed the contest."

"Here, he can have my ribbon," said Minnie, who had just won first prize for her pies.

So Commander got to wear a blue ribbon, too.

And he wore it very well!